The World's Most Amazing Structures

capstone
classroom

BTR Zone (Bridge to Reading) is published by Capstone Classroom,
1710 Roe Crest Drive, North Mankato, Minnesota 56003
www.capstoneclassroom.com

ISBN 978-1-62521-102-6

Editorial Credits
Brenda Haugen, editor; Ashlee Suker, designer; Eric Gohl, media researcher

Photo Credits
Alamy: ClassicStock, 36; BigStockPhoto.com: GoodMood Photo, 29, jboon,
14–15; Corbis: MAPS.com, 33; Dreamstime: Jose I. Soto, 44; NASA: 26, 56;
Newscom: Danita Delimont Photography/David Wall, 30, Getty Images/AFP/
Roslan Rahman, 47, KRT/Allen Holder, 12, 13, WENN/ZOB/CB2, cover, ZUMA
Press/Richard Ellis, 24; Shutterstock: Angelina Dimitrova, 18, Black Russian
Studio, 58–59, Boonsom, 34, cesc_assawin, 39, Horiyan, 22, Hung Chung
Chih, 40–41, imagemaker, 48, Jan-Dirk Hansen, 21, MACHKAZU, 53, Mazzzur,
8, nodff, 54, r.nagy, 7, Selfiy, 4, Songquan Deng, 50–51; Wikipedia: David
Monniaux, 42, Tom Corser, 10; Winchester Mystery House, San Jose, CA: 16, 17

Design Elements: Shutterstock

About the Cover
An Italian architect created plans for skyscrapers with floors that will rotate
up to once an hour.

Printed in the United States of America in North Mankato, Minnesota.
072015   009124R

TABLE OF —— CONTENTS

The Sydney Opera House hosts about 1,600 performances each year, including operas, ballets, concerts, and kids' shows.

tomb · a grave, room, or building that holds a dead body

architect · a person who designs and draws plans for buildings, bridges, and other construction projects

CHAPTER 1

Striking Structures

Amazing buildings are found all around the world. Some of these include giant skyscrapers, a hotel made of ice, and even an entire town built underground. Ancient **tombs** celebrate dead leaders. Huge theaters once held real-life fights to the death.

The Sydney Opera House

No other building looks quite like the Sydney Opera House. Some people say the roofs resemble giant sails in the harbor.

Architect Jørn Utzon's design was chosen for the Sydney Opera House in 1957. But in 1965, new leaders decided that they didn't like the interior designs that Utzon had planned. As a result, Utzon was forced to quit the project before it was finished.

The Sydney Opera House was supposed to open in 1963 at a cost of $7 million. But construction took 10 years longer than planned and cost almost 15 times as much as expected. It eventually opened in 1973 at a cost of $102 million.

Amazing Fact

Climber Alain Robert climbed the Sydney Opera House using only special sticky shoes in 1997.

Eiffel Tower

The Eiffel Tower opened in Paris, France, as the centerpiece of the World's Fair in 1889. It took several hundred workers more than two years to build the tower. It weighs 10,100 tons (9,163 metric tons) and contains 18,038 pieces of iron, which are held together by 2.5 million strong metal bolts called rivets.

At 984 feet (300 meters) high, the Eiffel Tower was the world's tallest structure when it opened. It held that honor until 1930 when the Chrysler Building in New York City surpassed it.

About 7 million people visit the Eiffel Tower each year. But when the tower was built, many people thought it was ugly. In fact, it was almost torn down in 1909. The monument was saved when its use as a radio tower was discovered. During World War I (1914–1918), the French used the Eiffel Tower to block enemy radio communication and win an important battle.

No Sale

A man named Victor Lustig "sold" the Eiffel Tower for **scrap metal** in 1925. He pretended that the government could not afford to keep the tower anymore. There was one major problem though. Lustig did not actually own the tower! A scrap metal dealer paid Lustig, who quickly escaped on a train carrying a suitcase full of cash. Lustig got away with the crime because the man who had "bought" the tower was too embarrassed to report Lustig to the police.

scrap metal · metal that can be recycled, normally by melting it down and using it to make a new metal object

Including the antenna at the top, the Eiffel Tower stands 1,063 feet (324 m) tall.

The highest part of the Taj Mahal is 561 feet (171 m) tall.

The Taj Mahal

Between 1632 and 1648, emperor Shah Jahan had the Taj Mahal built in Agra, India. He built the structure in memory of his wife, Mumtaz.

When he was just 15, Shah Jahan met Mumtaz Mahal. It was love at first sight for both of them. They quickly became inseparable.

Mumtaz gave birth to the couple's 14th child in 1631. But their joy quickly turned to sorrow when Mumtaz died from problems during childbirth. According to legend, with her dying breath Mumtaz asked Shah Jahan to build her a tomb more beautiful than anything else in the world. Six months later, he started building the Taj Mahal.

More than 1,000 elephants brought building materials from all over India and Asia for the Taj Mahal. About 20,000 workers constructed the building, which is known for its white marble exterior decorated with precious gems.

Shah Jahan died in 1666. He was buried in the Taj Mahal next to his beloved wife.

Amazing Fact
More than 2 million people visit the Taj Mahal each year.

The lobby of Sweden's ICEHOTEL

Chilling Out

- The outside temperature is a very cold −40°Fahrenheit (−40°Celsius). The temperature inside the hotel is around 23°F (−5°C).
- Some ice blocks weigh as much as 2 tons (1.8 metric tons).
- Reindeer skins cover the beds and doors to keep heat in.

Lapland · an area in northern Norway, Sweden, Finland, and Russia that falls within the Arctic Circle

CHAPTER 2

Unique and Unusual Structures

If every building was the same, the world would be a dull place. But there are many exciting buildings in the world. Some are even unusual.

The ICEHOTEL

An unusual hotel lies 125 miles (201 kilometers) north of the Arctic Circle in Sweden's **Lapland** region. What makes this structure so different? It is made almost entirely of ice and snow!

There are other ice hotels, but Sweden's ICEHOTEL is the oldest and largest. It opened in 1990 and boasts 64,000 square feet (5,946 square meters) of cool living space.

The ICEHOTEL must be rebuilt each winter. Ice artists come from around the world to help. They carve doors, windows, and sculptures. Even the beds and drinking glasses are made of ice!

The ICEHOTEL has a church where weddings take place and a theater where plays are performed. When the weather warms up in the spring, the hotel melts away.

Life in the Branches

A lot of children dream of having their own tree house. Out 'n' About Treehouse Treesort in southwestern Oregon is a vacation resort for anyone who loves tree houses.

The Treesort contains 18 tree houses—the largest group of tree houses in the world. A variety of tree houses were built to create this resort, including a pirate ship and a Western saloon. The highest tree house at the resort is 37 feet (11.3 m) off the ground.

The lower-level seating area in this tree house also converts into a sleeping area.

A walkway leads to a tree house.

People can even go to school at the Treehouse Institute of Takilma. This high school hangs from the branches of an oak tree.

Some walkways between the tree houses are up to 32 feet (9.8 m) off the ground and 90 feet (27.4 m) long. But a person can quickly get back to ground level by riding down a zip line.

13

Winchester Mystery House™

San Jose, California, may be home to the most unusual place in the United States—the Winchester Mystery House. Sarah Pardee was 22 years old when she married William Winchester in 1862. William's family owned the company that made Winchester rifles, which were very popular at the time. This company made William a rich man.

Even the roof design of the Winchester Mystery House is unusual.

After the deaths of her infant daughter and then William, Sarah was very sad. She went to see a medium, a person who claims to make contact with spirits of the dead. The medium said that the spirits of all the people who had been killed by Winchester rifles were haunting Sarah. The medium said that to make the spirits happy, Sarah needed to move out west and build a house for the spirits.

Sarah moved to San Jose in 1884 and started working on her house. Construction continued day and night for the next 38 years, until Sarah died in 1922.

The nonstop hammering resulted in one bizarre building. The enormous house has 24,000 square feet (2,230 square meters) of living space. That's about the size of 13 average homes! It is believed that over time, 500 to 600 rooms were built, but some were torn down or rebuilt. The house now has 160 rooms, including 40 bedrooms and 13 bathrooms. It also has 47 fireplaces, six kitchens, and 467 doorways. One of the home's 40 staircases has steps that are each only 2 inches (5 centimeters) high. Another staircase goes down seven steps then up 11.

This staircase leads visitors down to another staircase that goes up.

The unusual home also has several secret passageways, as well as doors that lead nowhere and open into walls. According to legend, Sarah put all of these quirks into her mansion to confuse the spirits she believed were out to get her.

With the home's peculiar history, it's no surprise that it's said to be haunted. Many

The staircase with 2-inch (5-cm) stairs

people have heard strange noises, such as organ music, footsteps, and banging doors. Others say they have seen doorknobs turning by themselves.

Amazing Fact

After her husband died, Sarah's **inheritance** gave her an income of about $1,000 a day. That would be about $30,000 a day in today's money! At the time, the average salary was about $750 per year.

inheritance · property or money one person receives after another person has died

17

The Tower Bridge roadway rises to let a boat pass underneath.

walkways · a path or passage for walking

CHAPTER 3

Breathtaking Bridges

By design, bridges are amazing structures. Many of them are miles long, crossing bodies of water or steep land with few supports to hold them up. Some connect cities or countries, some cut travel times drastically, and some are just cool to see.

London's Tower Bridge

Tower Bridge is one of the oldest and most famous bridges in the world. It is 880 feet (268 m) long and spans the River Thames in London, England. The bridge was made out of steel and stone. Two stone towers in the central part of the bridge are each 200 feet (61 m) tall.

Tower Bridge was finished in 1894. It was built to ease the traffic problems in London at the time. The bridge was built for both vehicles and people who are walking. A road runs across the bottom level of the bridge. People who are walking use two glass-covered **walkways** that stretch between the two towers. The bridge's roadway can be raised to allow boats to travel beneath it.

Golden Gate Bridge

The Golden Gate Bridge in San Francisco, California, is one of the most recognizable bridges in the world. It is named for the Golden Gate Strait, the body of water that connects San Francisco Bay to the Pacific Ocean. The bridge is painted orange so that passing ships can see it better at night and in the fog.

In May 1937, the Golden Gate Bridge was opened. It took four years to build it, cost $35 million, and took the lives of 11 workers.

The Golden Gate is a **suspension bridge**. Thick cables hold up the roadway. The cables are anchored to two tall towers.

suspension bridge · a bridge with a roadway suspended from two or more cables usually passing over towers and strongly anchored at the ends

The bridge is 1.7 miles (2.7 km) long and 220 feet (67 m) high at the midway point. The two main cables, which are also at the midpoint, are 746 feet (227 m) high. Since the bridge opened, more than 2 million vehicles have crossed it.

Amazing Fact

A safety net installed under the Golden Gate Bridge during construction saved the lives of 19 workers.

Today the Golden Gate Bridge would cost more than $1.2 billion to build.

The Akashi-Kaikyo Bridge is also known as the Pearl Bridge.

Akashi-Kaikyo Bridge

The Akashi-Kaikyo Bridge in Kobe, Japan, is the longest and tallest suspension bridge in the world. It is 2.4 miles (4 km) long. Its two towers are the highest of any bridge in the world at 928 feet (283 m) tall. The Akashi-Kaikyo Bridge took 2 million workers more than 10 years to build.

The bridge spans a very busy sea route. More than 1,000 ships pass beneath the bridge each day. For that reason, it was built with as few supports as possible so that ships can easily pass under it.

The bridge was also built to withstand high winds and strong earthquakes. During the bridge's construction, a powerful earthquake rocked Kobe, Japan, testing the bridge's design to its limits.

Amazing Fact

If stretched end to end, the cables used on the Akashi-Kaikyo Bridge could circle Earth seven and a half times!

A guest at Jules Undersea Lodge goes through a doorway into his bedroom.

CHAPTER 4

Below Ground

Living underground is not a new idea. Cave people were doing it thousands of years ago. But these days underground—or even underwater—living can be an exciting choice to life above ground.

Jules Undersea Lodge

Many people wonder what it would be like to live underwater. Now they can find out at Jules Undersea Lodge in Key Largo, Florida.

Jules Undersea Lodge started out as a research lab. Research projects are still conducted there, but in 1986 it also became the world's first underwater hotel. The hotel is built upon **stilts** that are 5 feet (1.5 m) off of a **lagoon** floor.

To get to the lodge, guests must dive 21 feet (6.4 m) below the surface of the ocean. Ocean life such as sea horses, puffer fish, manatees, and barracudas surround the hotel.

stilt · a post that holds up a building
lagoon · a shallow area of water

Aquarius

Aquarius is the only underwater research lab in the world. It serves as a temporary home to scientists or **aquanauts** who want to investigate life in the ocean. *Aquarius* is currently located near Key Largo, Florida. However, because it can be moved, it could be sent to explore other areas of the ocean in the future.

Aquarius rests 63 feet (19 m) underwater.

Aquarius allows aquanauts to live and work underwater on missions that can last up to two weeks. This lab saves time and money because aquanauts do not have to return to the surface after each dive. Divers enter and leave *Aquarius* through a wet porch, which is a room with a hole in floor. The air pressure inside *Aquarius* stops water from coming in. When people want to leave, they just jump through the hole and swim away!

Aquarius offers researchers all the comforts of home. It has enough beds for six people as well as bathrooms, a microwave, a refrigerator, and computer workstations.

Amazing Fact

Aquarius survived the destruction caused by hurricanes Katrina and Rita in 2005.

aquanaut · a scuba diver who lives and works inside and outside an underwater shelter for an extended period

Living Underground

For thousands of years, caves and dugout homes have been used for shelter. Although underground houses are not as common today, these homes are gaining popularity.

Underground houses are built entirely below the surface of the earth. An earth-sheltered home is often dug into the side of a hill or mountain. It is surrounded by earth on three sides. Both types of homes use less energy than traditional aboveground homes.

The temperature of the soil naturally keeps these homes warmer during winter and cooler during summer. This is because Earth's **mass** retains a more consistent temperature. As a result, heating and cooling costs are much lower in these types of homes.

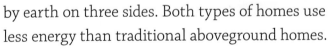

mass · the amount of material in an object

An underground home built under a hill

Underground homes are very quiet. They also are safer when severe weather strikes, especially tornadoes. Besides, it's just plain cool to live in a house where you can mow the lawn or plant a garden on your roof!

Coober Pedy

To take shelter from the summer heat, people in Coober Pedy, Australia, began using old mines as houses. Soon homes, restaurants, shops, and churches were being built underground in the desert town. Today more than half of the people of Coober Pedy live underground.

The lobby of a hotel in Coober Pedy was once part of a mine.

Coober Pedy has a unique **landscape** that resembles the surface of the moon or a distant planet. **Opals** were discovered in Coober Pedy in 1916. Since then, people have been mining the areas to collect the opals. There are now more than 250,000 old mines. It can be dangerous to walk around the area, because the ground is weak and full of holes from old mines.

In Cooper Pedy, nighttime temperatures can drop below freezing (32°F/0°C) during the winter. Daytime temperatures in the summer can reach 122°F (50°C) or higher. But the underground buildings stay comfortable. They have an average temperature of 70°F (21°C) to 79°F (26°C).

landscape · the form of the land in a particular area

opal · a mineral with changeable colors that is used as a gem

31

The Chunnel

The Channel Tunnel, or "Chunnel" as it is known, is an **engineering** marvel. It connects the countries of England and France beneath the English Channel waterway. High-speed trains carry more than 16 million passengers through the Chunnel each year.

Construction began on the Chunnel in 1988. Workers used huge drills to create tunnels in the chalky earth.It took 13,000 workers six years to dig the 95 miles (153 km) of tunnels. The Chunnel cost $21 billion.

The Chunnel is actually made up of three main tunnels. The tunnels are 24 miles (38.6 km) underwater at their deepest points. Each tunnel is about 31.4 miles (50.5 km) long. Two tunnels are for trains traveling in each direction. The middle one serves as an emergency escape route.

At speeds of 100 miles (161 km) per hour, trains zip underneath the English Channel in just 20 minutes. The same trip takes almost two hours by ferryboat.

engineering · the use of science to design structures

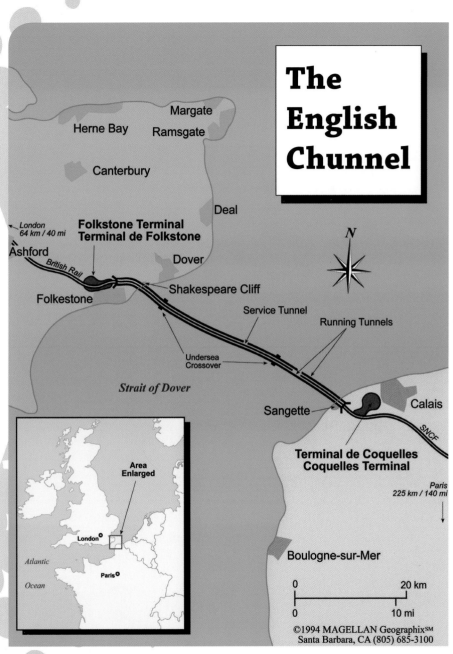

The English Chunnel

- Margate
- Herne Bay
- Ramsgate
- Canterbury
- Deal
- London 64 km / 40 mi
- **Folkstone Terminal / Terminal de Folkstone**
- Ashford
- British Rail
- Dover
- Shakespeare Cliff
- Folkestone
- Service Tunnel
- Running Tunnels
- Undersea Crossover
- *Strait of Dover*
- Sangette
- Calais
- SNCF
- **Terminal de Coquelles / Coquelles Terminal**
- Paris 225 km / 140 mi
- Boulogne-sur-Mer

N

Inset map
- Area Enlarged
- London
- Atlantic Ocean
- Paris

Scale: 0 — 20 km / 0 — 10 mi

©1994 MAGELLAN Geographix℠
Santa Barbara, CA (805) 685-3100

At its lowest point, the Chunnel sits 250 feet (76 m) below sea level.

The Great Pyramid

CHAPTER 5

Ancient Wonders

Modern buildings are awe-inspiring due to their ever-increasing heights and creative design features. But ancient structures are even more amazing because they were built without the aid of modern technology. And they have stood the test of time. Some have lasted for thousands of years.

The Great Pyramid at Giza

Throughout Egypt's scorching desert lie more than 100 pyramids. The most famous of these is the Great Pyramid of Giza. As the last remaining of the Seven Wonders of the Ancient World, the pyramid is roughly 4,500 years old. For almost 4,000 of those years, it was the tallest building on Earth at 455 feet (139 m) high.

It took about 20 years to build the Great Pyramid. This massive structure is made of about 2.3 million limestone blocks. Each block weighs between 2.5 and 15 tons (2.3 and 13.6 metric tons).

Workers pushed blocks to a site where a pyramid was being built.

How much does the pyramid weigh?

The Great Pyramid weighs about 6.5 million tons (6 million metric tons). That's about the same as:

- one million tyrannosaurus rex dinosaurs, or
- 48,000 blue whales, or
- 3.25 million automobiles.

Nearly 100,000 workers rolled and transported the blocks to the site. Then they lifted the blocks onto the structure using ropes and pulleys. Some of the heaviest blocks were brought from 500 miles (805 km) away. The Great Pyramid took about 23 years to complete.

The pyramid contains several rooms that were built to protect the tombs of Egyptian rulers. Mountains of gold and jewels were stored in these hidden chambers. Secret passageways, dead ends, and disguised doorways were built to discourage thieves. Yet robbers still managed to get inside and steal some of the treasure.

But robbers didn't take all of the treasure. **Archaeologists** have found jewelry, paintings, and weapons. Archaeologists also have found the remains of humans and animals.

archaeologist · a scientist who studies how people lived in the past

The Colosseum

The Colosseum in Rome, Italy, is the largest **amphitheater** in the world. It was built nearly 2,000 years ago, around 80 A.D., for public entertainment. It could hold 50,000 people.

Back then, people wanted to see gladiators, men who fought one another to the death. Men also fought wild beasts. Plays, gladiator contests, and reenactments of battles were often held at the Colosseum. Sometimes the building was flooded with water so that mock sea battles could be staged.

The Colosseum is 612 feet (187 m) long, 515 feet (157 m) wide, and 157 feet (48 m) tall. It is made of stone and concrete and has many underground tunnels, which were used to house wild animals. These animals would suddenly be let loose from trap doors to join in the battles.

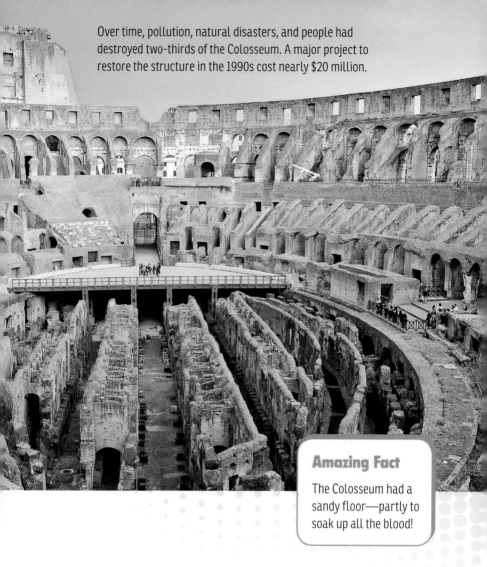

Over time, pollution, natural disasters, and people had destroyed two-thirds of the Colosseum. A major project to restore the structure in the 1990s cost nearly $20 million.

Amazing Fact

The Colosseum had a sandy floor—partly to soak up all the blood!

The Colosseum is a reminder of Rome's long history. Today it is one of the city's most popular tourist attractions. Millions of people visit this amazing structure each year.

amphitheater · a large, open-air building with rows of seats in a high circle around an arena

The Great Wall of China

At 5,500 miles (8,851 km) long, the Great Wall of China is the longest structure on Earth made by humans. For centuries, the Chinese had used walls to protect their cities and lands. But the walls were old, worn, and spread out. Some dated back to the 7th century B.C.

More than 2,200 years ago, in 214 B.C., emperor Qin Shi Huangdi wanted the walls connected to make one great wall. This wall would be longer, taller, and stronger to defend against enemies.

Hundreds of thousands of people worked on the Great Wall. On average, the wall is 25 feet (7.6 m) high and 20 feet (6 m) wide. Along most sections, a 13-foot- (4-m-) wide roadway runs along the top of the wall.

Amazing Fact

The Badaling is one of the most visited sections of the Great Wall. It is famous for the way the wall snakes up and down mountain slopes.

More than 10 million tourists visit the Great Wall each year. Depending on what part is visited, the wall may be broken or in ruins. Over the years, **vandals** have damaged many parts of the wall. Other parts have been knocked down for new construction projects. People have even stolen bricks to build their own homes.

vandal · a person who destroys or damages property on purpose

A portion of the Great Wall of China

The library in Hearst Castle

CHAPTER 6

Magnificent Castles and Palaces

Castles and palaces are among the grandest buildings in the world. Some serve as royal homes or government offices. Others are now museums. Whatever their uses, castles and palaces are some of the most amazing structures in the world.

Hearst Castle

Publisher William Randolph Hearst inherited 250,000 acres (101,171 hectares) of land near San Simeon, California, in 1919. He decided to build a small house there, but he ended up building an American castle.

Hearst Castle sits on a hilltop about 1,600 feet (488 m) high. By 1947 the castle contained 165 rooms, including 56 bedrooms. It also had a movie theater, tennis courts, a private airport, indoor and outdoor swimming pools, and the world's largest private zoo.

Hearst died in 1951, before his castle was fully completed. But since 1957, Hearst Castle has been a popular place for tourists to visit.

The Palace of Versailles

The Palace of Versailles began as a royal hunting lodge about 20 miles (32 km) southwest of Paris, France. In 1661 King Louis XIV began turning it into one of the largest and most spectacular palaces in the world.

The king wanted grand apartments for himself and the queen. He also wanted homes for various members of the French government. The project almost **bankrupted** the government.

The Hall of Mirrors is one of the most famous rooms in the Palace of Versailles.

Amazing Fact

The Treaty of Versailles, which ended World War I, was signed in the Hall of Mirrors in 1919.

Louis and his **successors** continued to add on to the palace. It now has 700 rooms and can hold up to 20,000 people. The most magnificent room at Versailles is the Hall of Mirrors. This room is decorated with 578 mirrors placed on walls opposite the windows so they reflect the sunlight. Dazzling chandeliers dangle from the 40-foot (12-m) ceiling, which is painted with scenes from the reign of Louis XIV.

After the **French Revolution** in the late 1700s, Versailles was no longer the center of government. Today it is a popular tourist attraction, and it remains one of the grandest palaces in history.

bankrupt · unable to pay debts

successor · one who follows, usually in line to a royal or government position

French Revolution · from 1789 to 1799, when the government of France changed many times; people disagreed about how France should be ruled, because ordinary people wanted more power and more rights

Istana Nurul Iman

Istana Nurul Iman is the official home of the **Sultan** of Brunei and is the center of the nation's government. Brunei is a small country in Southeast Asia, but the sultan's palace is the largest home in the world. At more than 2 million square feet (185,806 square meters), it's so large that 1,200 average-sized homes could fit inside it.

Surrounded by beautiful gardens and topped with a golden dome, the sultan's palace was built in 1984 and cost more than $350 million. It boasts 1,788 rooms, 257 bathrooms, five swimming pools, and a 110-car garage. It also has a **mosque** that can hold up to 1,500 people. It even has air-conditioned stables for 200 ponies.

The throne room in Istana Nural Iman

sultan · a king or ruler especially of a Muslim state
mosque · a building used by Muslims for worship

Because Istana Nurul Iman is a private home, it isn't open for tours. However, for three days per year, the royal family opens the home's doors to the public. During that time, 10,000 lucky visitors get to explore inside the palace. They might even get to meet the sultan himself.

Amazing Fact

In Arabic, Istana Nurul Iman means "palace of the light of faith."

A skywalk connects the Petronas Towers on their 42nd floors.

CHAPTER 7

High Up in the Sky

Skyscrapers are part of the everyday landscape in big cities. The Home Insurance Building in Chicago, Illinois, was the first skyscraper. It was only 138 feet (42 m) tall when it was built in 1884. Today the world's tallest skyscraper soars an amazing 2,717 feet (828 m) into the air!

Petronas Towers

The Petronas Towers in Kuala Lumpur, Malaysia, were the world's tallest skyscrapers from 1996 to 2003. The towers are 1,483 feet (452 m) tall with 88 floors. The buildings are made of concrete, steel, and glass.

The Petronas Towers are two skyscrapers connected by a skywalk. The skywalk has a viewing area that is open to the public.

These skyscrapers reflected the growth of the Malaysian economy when they were built. An economy is the way a country handles its money and resources. The Petronas Towers are used mainly as offices, with a shopping mall on the ground floor.

Willis Tower

At 1,450 feet (442 m), the Willis Tower in Chicago was the tallest building in the United States for 40 years. It was the world's tallest building for 23 years until that record was taken over by the Petronas Towers.

Originally known as the Sears Tower, the 110-story building took three years to build and was completed in 1973. The Willis Tower contains enough concrete to make a 5-mile (8-km) long freeway with eight lanes!

The states of Illinois, Indiana, Michigan, and Wisconsin are often visible from an observation deck on the 103rd floor. An all-glass balcony was added to the observation deck in 2009. This clear ledge allows daring visitors to look through the floor and gaze down at the city streets 1,353 feet (412 m) below.

Amazing Fact

Alain Robert, who calls himself the "French Spiderman," climbed the Willis Tower using only his bare hands and feet in 1999. It took him just over an hour. When he reached the top, he was quickly arrested.

The Willis Tower has more than 25 miles (40 km) of plumbing, 80 miles (129 km) of elevator cable, and 145,000 light fixtures.

Taipei 101

Taipei 101 was the world's tallest building from 2003 until 2007. It is 1,670 feet (509 m) tall and has 101 floors. It is designed to stay standing in typhoon winds and earthquakes. The building is supported by 36 mega columns filled with concrete.

A large, very heavy ball called a tuned mass damper hangs inside Taipei 101. It helps to keep the building from swaying in high winds or during an earthquake. It works like a pendulum, swinging in the opposite direction of the movement of the building.

Taipei 101 was based on classic Chinese design. It is shaped like a pagoda, a traditional Asian building. In China and Taiwan, the number eight is thought to be lucky, so the building has eight tiers (layers), and each tier has eight stories.

Taipei 101 is used for many different things. Offices occupy 77 of the floors. The other floors house restaurants, stores, and a two-floor gym. A station for the Taipei Mass Rapid Transit train is located underneath the building.

Amazing Fact

The sectioned tower was inspired by the bamboo plant, a Chinese symbol of strength, endurance, and elegance. Taipei 101 also has four circles near the base that represent coins. It is hoped that these circles will bring success to any businesses that operate in the building.

Taipei 101 soars above the surrounding buildings in Taipei, Taiwan.

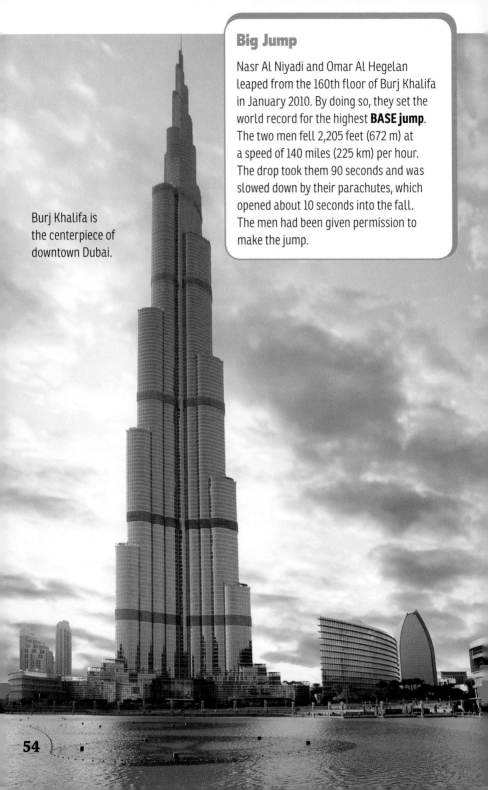

Big Jump

Nasr Al Niyadi and Omar Al Hegelan leaped from the 160th floor of Burj Khalifa in January 2010. By doing so, they set the world record for the highest **BASE jump**. The two men fell 2,205 feet (672 m) at a speed of 140 miles (225 km) per hour. The drop took them 90 seconds and was slowed down by their parachutes, which opened about 10 seconds into the fall. The men had been given permission to make the jump.

Burj Khalifa is the centerpiece of downtown Dubai.

Burj Khalifa

While still under construction in 2007, Burj Khalifa became the world's tallest skyscraper when it surpassed Taipei 101 in height. Completed in 2010, Burj Khalifa in Dubai, United Arab Emirates, stands at an amazing 2,717 feet (828 m). Offices, luxury homes, a hotel, and four swimming pools can be found inside building. It has 162 floors and cost about $1.5 billion to build.

About 11.6 million cubic feet (328,000 cubic meters) of concrete were used to build Burj Khalifa. The foundation of the massive building extends 164 feet (50 m) below the ground. A unique steel cone provides support for the building and keeps it from twisting.

Burj Khalifa is so huge that the water produced from the air-conditioning system could fill 20 Olympic-sized swimming pools each year. But the water isn't wasted. It's used to water the large gardens that surround the tower.

BASE jump · to parachute from a tall building, tower, bridge, gorge, or mountain; BASE stands for Building, Antenna, Span, and Earth

International Space Station

The International Space Station (ISS) hovers in orbit about 240 miles (386 km) above Earth. The first section was launched into space in 1998. Its first crew arrived there in October 2000.

The ISS is about the size of an American football field, and it cost about $100 billion to build. It was designed as a place for scientists to carry out experiments on space and how living there affects the human body.

The ISS is bigger than a five-bedroom house.

Astronauts from 15 different countries, including the United States, Russia, Canada, Japan, and the United Kingdom, have visited the ISS. It travels a whopping 15,500 mph (24,945 kph) and orbits Earth almost 16 times a day. In its first 10 years, the ISS traveled more than 1.5 billion miles (2.4 billion km). If it had been traveling in a straight line instead of circling Earth, the ISS would be past Pluto and at the edge of our solar system by now.

Freedom Tower

One World Trade Center, nicknamed the Freedom Tower, is the tallest building in the United States at 1,776 feet (541 m). It was built in New York City on the site of the Twin Towers, which were destroyed during the terrorist attacks on September 11, 2001. The Twin Towers included World Trade Center Tower One and World Trade Center Tower Two.

The bulding has 104 floors.

The building has 69 floors of offices and two restaurants.

The cost to build the tower topped out at more than $3.8 billion.

The Freedom Tower will collect rainwater and use it to water the surrounding park.
The building also plans to use 30 percent less water and 20 percent less energy than other buildings in New York City.

SPIRE—408 feet (124 m) tall; weighs more than 700 tons (635 metric tons)

The roof reaches 1,368 feet (417 m) high, the height of World Trade Center Tower One.

The observation deck is at 1,362 feet (415 m), the height of World Trade Center Tower Two, which was destroyed on September 11, 2001.

Read More

Bingham, Jane. *Architecture*. Culture in Action. Chicago: Raintree, 2009.

Brasch, Nicolas. *Triumphs of Engineering*. Discovery Education: Techology. New York: PowerKids Press, 2013.

Farrell, Courtney. *Build It Green*. Let's Explore Science. Vero Beach, Fla.: Rourke Publishing Group, 2010.

Graham, Ian. *Gigantic Lengths and Other Vast Megastructures*. Megastructures. Mankato, Minn.: QEB Publishing, 2012.

Hurley, Michael. *The World's Most Amazing Skyscrapers*. Landmark Top Tens. Chicago: Raintree, 2012.

Kerns, Ann. *Seven Wonders of Architecture*. Minneapolis: Twenty-First Century Books, 2010.

Solway, Andrew. *Civil Engineering and the Science of Structures*. Engineering in Action. St. Catharines, Ontario: Crabtree Publishing Company, 2013.

Internet Sites

FactHound offers a safe, fun way to find Internet sites related to this book. All of the sites on FactHound have been researched by our staff.

Here's all you do:
Visit *www.facthound.com*
Type in this code: 9781625211026

Check out projects, games and lots more at
www.capstonekids.com

Glossary
of Text Features

Text Feature	How to Use It
Caption: A word or group of words shown with a picture or illustration	Read a caption to understand information that may not be in the text.
Diagram: A drawing that shows or explains something	Examine a diagram to understand steps in a process, how something is made, or the parts of something.
Glossary: List of key terms with their meanings	Look up key terms in the glossary to find their meanings and to get a better understanding of the topic of the text.
Index: Alphabetical list of key terms, names, and topics in a text with their page numbers	Use the index to find pages that contain information you are looking for.
Map: A drawing that represents a place, such as a country or city	Use a map to understand relative locations and determine where events took place.
Photograph or Illustration: Visuals that are created by cameras or drawn	Examine photographs and illustrations to better understand ideas in the text that might be unclear.
Subhead: Word or group of words that divides the text into sections and tells the main idea of a section	Use subheads to locate information in the text and understand how a text is organized.
Table: Represents data in a small space	Examine a table to understand data or to compare information in the text.
Table of Contents: List of the major parts of the book and their page numbers	Use a table of contents to locate general information in the text and see how the topics are organized.
Text Box: A box in the text that provides extra information about a topic	Read a text box to understand interesting or important information.
Text Style: Bold, color, or italic words in the text	Pay attention to bold, italic, and color words to figure out which words in the text are important.
Timeline: Shows events in the order in which they occurred	Use a timeline to understand the order in which events occurred or how one event led to another.

Glossary

amphitheater (AM-fuh-thee-uh-tuhr) · a large, open-air building with rows of seats in a high circle around an arena

aquanaut (UH-kwaw-nawt) · a scuba diver who lives and works inside and outside an underwater shelter for an extended period

archaeologist (ar-kee-AH-luh-jist) · a scientist who studies how people lived in the past

architect (AR-ki-tekt) · a person who designs and draws plans for buildings, bridges, and other construction projects

bankrupt (BANG-kruhpt) · unable to pay debts

BASE jump (BAYS JUHMP) · to parachute from a tall building, tower, bridge, gorge, or mountain; BASE stands for Building, Antenna, Span, and Earth

engineering (en-juh-NEER-ing) · the use of science to design structures

French Revolution (FRENCH rev-uh-LOO-shuhn) · from 1789 to 1799, when the government of France changed many times; people disagreed about how France should be ruled, because ordinary people wanted more power and more rights

inheritance (in-HAYR-uh-tuhnss) · property or money one person receives after another person has died

lagoon (luh-GOON) · a shallow area of water

landscape (LAND-skayp) · the form of the land in a particular area

Lapland (LAP-lahnd) • an area in northern Norway, Sweden, Finland, and Russia that falls within the Arctic Circle

mass (MASS) • the amount of material in an object

mosque (MOSK) • a building used by Muslims for worship

opal (OH-puhl) • a mineral with changeable colors that is used as a gem

scrap metal (SKRAP MET-uhl) • metal that can be recycled, normally by melting it down and using it to make a new metal object

stilt (STILT) • a post that holds up a building

successor (suhk-SEH-suhr) • one who follows, usually in line to a royal or government position

sultan (SUHL-tuhn) • a king or ruler especially of a Muslim state

suspension bridge (suh-SPEN-shuhn BRIDJ) • a bridge with a roadway suspended from two or more cables usually passing over towers and strongly anchored at the ends

tomb (TOOM) • a grave, room, or building that holds a dead body

vandal (VAN-duhl) • a person who destroys or damages property on purpose

walkway (WAWK-way) • a path or passage for walking

Index